Magic Animal Friends

For Darcie Littley

Special thanks to Valerie Wilding

ORCHARD BOOKS

First published in Great Britain in 2014 by The Watts Publishing Group
This edition published in 2017 by The Watts Publishing Group

5

A CIP catalogue record for this book is available from the British Library.

ISBN 978 1 40834 842 0

Printed in Great Britain by Clays Ltd, Elcograf S.p.A.

MIX
Paper from responsible sources
FSC® C104740
FSC www.fsc.org

The paper and board used in this book are made from wood from responsible sources

Orchard Books
An imprint of Hachette Children's Group
Part of The Watts Publishing Group Limited
Carmelite House, 50 Victoria Embankment, London EC4Y 0DZ

An Hachette UK Company
www.hachette.co.uk
www.hachettechildrens.co.uk

Lucy Longwhiskers Gets Lost

Daisy Meadows

ORCHARD

Shining House
Sunshine Meadow
Blossom Briar
Toadstool Cafe
Goldie's Grotto
Toadstool Glade
Mrs Taptree's Library
Library
Friendship Tree
Maze
Silver Spring
Buttercup Grove
Lighthouse

Map of Friendship Forest

Can you keep a secret? I thought you could!
Then I'll tell you about an enchanted wood.
It lies through the door in the old oak tree,
Let's go there now - just follow me!
We'll find adventure that never ends,
And meet the Magic Animal Friends!

Love

Goldie the Cat

Contents

CHAPTER ONE

A Golden Visitor

Lily Hart stepped into the long garden, breathing in the scent of the dewy grass. In the distance, nestled behind a copse of trees, was the barn her parents had turned into the Helping Paw Wildlife Hospital. Lily shrugged a sleeveless cardigan over her stripy green dress, then picked up the bucket of lettuce leaves waiting by the back door. Swinging it over her arm, she walked over to a large run with a wire fence. At the end of the run was a wooden hutch.

"Breakfast time!" Lily called. A pink, whiskery nose poked out from one of the hutch's doors, then another. Soon three rabbits were hopping towards Lily. Two of them had bandages on their paws and the other had a bandage over its ear.

Lily opened the top of the run and tipped the lettuce leaves into a bowl.

"Eat up," she murmured. Her bobbed dark hair had fallen across her face and Lily tucked it behind an ear as she watched the rabbits nibble the leaves. *They're nearly better now*, she thought. *They'll soon be ready to go back to their burrow.*

A flash of movement from the row of houses across the lane caught Lily's eye. One of the front doors had opened, and out came a blonde girl in denim shorts, leggings and a pink hoodie.

Lily smiled. It was Jess Forester – her best friend!

Jess checked that the lane was clear and hurried to the garden gate. She grinned as Lily ran to meet her.

"First day of the holidays!" said Jess as the two friends hugged. "You know what would make this summer extra amazing? Helping in the hospital every day!"

Like Lily, Jess adored animals, and she loved living opposite the Hart family.

Lily clapped her hands together. "Then let's get started! I've just fed the rabbits, but the other animals need their breakfasts, too."

The girls passed the copse of trees where the Harts kept injured deer. A fawn was skipping around happily on three legs. His fourth leg was wrapped in a plaster cast.

"Dad fixed his leg yesterday," Lily explained. "I helped."

"Looks like you did a good job!" Jess patted the pocket of her shorts, where she kept her mini-sketchbook and pencil. "I'll have to draw him later."

They entered the barn, smelling the clean hay and fresh sawdust.

Mrs Hart was standing by a hutch. "Just the helpers I need!" she said with a smile. Her jeans were tucked into a pair of muddy wellies, and her dark hair was piled into a messy bun. "Could you feed these fox cubs for me?" she asked. "The poor things were found all alone."

Lily fetched two pairs of thick gloves and Jess fished in her pocket for a hairband to tie back her blonde curls. They were ready for work!

Soon the fox cubs were drinking greedily from feeding bottles, just like babies! When they'd finished, Lily entered the feed time in the hospital's computer.

"Can you fill the water bottles in the hutches, please?" asked Mrs Hart. "All except the end one – that hutch is empty. I'm off to check the baby badgers. They're very happy in the sett we built. They seem to think it's a real one!" She bustled out of the barn.

Lily and Jess filled the bottles from little watering cans, speaking softly to the squirrels, mice and hedgehogs as they worked.

Finally Jess said, "That's the lot."

But suddenly Lily saw something move in the end hutch. *Funny*, she thought. *Mum said it was empty*.

"Look, Jess," she whispered, opening the door and peering inside.

In the shadows at the back of the hutch nestled a cat. Its pointed ears twitched at

the sight of the girls.

"That's weird," said Jess. "How did a cat get in?"

"Magic?" suggested Lily. They both laughed.

With a mew, the cat leaped out of the hutch. It had golden fur and eyes as green as spring leaves.

"She's so pretty," said Jess, tickling the soft fur on the cat's head. "Lily, doesn't she look just like that cat who came in last year with the hurt paw?"

Lily looked thoughtfully at the cat. "She

does! I wonder if it's her. Let's check."

Lily went to the computer to check the patient records. She clicked through a few pages, then gasped.

"Look!" she said, pointing to an old entry on the screen. It read:

Patient: Female cat.

Appearance: Gold fur, green eyes.

No collar – maybe a stray?

Notes: Arrived with an injured paw. Healed well. Took a real shine to Lily and Jess! Patient then disappeared.

Beneath the entry was a photograph of the golden cat.

"We were right!" said Jess. "I wonder why she's come back today?"

The cat jumped down from the hutch and curled around the girls' legs, purring.

"She doesn't look sick," said Lily, "so that can't be the reason. It's a mystery!"

The cat moved towards the barn door, stopped and looked back at the girls, then darted outside!

"Come on!" called Jess. "Let's catch that cat – before she disappears again!"

CHAPTER TWO

The Magical Tree

Lily and Jess ran outside. The golden cat sprinted across the Harts' lawn towards Brightley Stream, which ran along the bottom of the garden.

"That's weird," Jess panted as the girls followed. "Cats usually keep away from water."

Lily's dad had put stepping stones in the stream so people could cross safely. The cat sprang onto the first stepping stone. Then she looked over her shoulder at the girls and mewed.

Lily's dark eyes were wide. "She isn't running away," Lily said. "I think she wants us to follow her!"

With a flick of her golden tail, the cat leaped onto the next stone. The girls

quickly jumped after her. On the other side of the stream, in Brightley Meadow, stood a huge oak tree. Even though it was the middle of summer, the tree had no leaves. Jess's dad was a science teacher, and he'd told them it was dead.

But as the cat ran to the tree, something amazing happened. Leaves sprang from every twig, bright green and shimmering in the sunshine, as if they had been

speckled with gold dust. Birds swooped down to the branches and began singing, and bumblebees and butterflies danced among the yellow flowers below.

"It's come back to life!" Lily said with a

gasp. "How is that possible?"

Jess rubbed her eyes. She couldn't believe what they were seeing!

The golden cat was rubbing around the tree trunk, pawing at some strange marks.

Jess kneeled to stroke her silky fur. "I know this sounds crazy, but I think the cat has something to do with this!"

Lily nodded, her eyes wide. "Look! There's writing carved into the trunk."

Jess crawled round the tree, reading the letters. "Friend…ship...For…est…"

The cat mewed and pawed at the letters once more.

"Maybe she wants us to say it louder?" Jess guessed. "FRIENDSHIP FOREST!" she shouted.

But the cat just mewed again. She rubbed first Lily's leg, then Jess's, and pawed at the letters.

"I know!" cried Lily. "She wants us to read it together!"

Both girls said, "Friendship Forest!"

Instantly, a small door appeared in the trunk! It was as high as the girls' shoulders and in the centre was a handle shaped like a leaf.

"Wow!" said Jess. Her eyes shone as she

gripped the handle.

Lily reached towards it too, then hesitated. "Do you think we should open it?" she asked warily. "We don't know what's on the other side."

"Exactly!" said Jess with a grin. "Let's find out!"

Lily twisted the handle, and the little door swung open. A shimmering golden light poured out of the tree.

The cat looked up at the girls. Her green eyes seemed to beg them to follow, then she bounded inside the tree.

Jess held out her hand to Lily. "Ready?" she asked with a smile.

Lily grinned and took Jess's hand. "Let's go!"

Taking a deep breath, they bent down. As they squeezed through the door, their skin tingled all over.

The girls blinked as the golden glow faded. They were standing in a clearing in the middle of a sunlit forest.

The leaves on the tall trees shimmered and flowers nodded their colourful heads in the gentle breeze. The ground was covered in soft, springy moss.

"This is impossible," Jess said. "How can all this fit inside a tree trunk?"

Lily took Jess's hand again. She was trembling with excitement. "There is an explanation for all this..."

Jess nodded. Together, both girls cried, "Magic!"

"This is amazing!" Jess said, grinning. "But why did the cat bring us here?" She glanced around. "Where's she gone?"

Lily peered behind some pink flowers with petals like tissue paper, hoping to catch a glimpse of golden fur. A familiar scent drifted up from the blooms.

"These smell like candyfloss!" she exclaimed. "Even the flowers are magical!" Then something odd caught her eye.

Inside a hollowed-out tree trunk stood a little cottage.

"Look!" Lily cried.

"Sweet!" said Jess. "But what's a play house doing here?"

A curtain at one of the windows twitched. Jess shook her head. Surely there couldn't be anyone inside the cottage... Could there?

As the girls gazed around, their eyes widened. More little cottages were dotted around the clearing. Some were nestled among tree roots, and one was half underground, with a mossy roof. Tables and chairs as high as the girls' knees stood outside a wooden cabin with white spots on the roof. A sign said *Toadstool Café*.

A door at the side of the café suddenly slammed shut. From inside came the sound of worried voices.

Lily gasped. "Someone's living in these little buildings," she said. "But who?"

CHAPTER THREE

Friendship Forest

"They're the animals of Friendship Forest," said a voice.

The girls turned around, trying to work out where the voice had come from. To their astonishment, they saw that the golden cat had reappeared. Standing upright on her hind legs, she reached

almost to the girls' shoulders – and she was smiling at them! Jess noticed that she had a glittery scarf looped around her neck, too.

After a few moments, Jess found her voice. "You can talk," she said, shaking her head in amazement. "And you've grown!"

The cat laughed, her green eyes sparkling. "Actually, you two have shrunk! You became smaller when you stepped through the door in the tree," she said.

"Oh, so that's what the tingling feeling was!" said Jess.

The cat nodded. "My name's Goldie. Welcome to Friendship Forest, Jess and Lily!"

Lily gasped. "You know our names!"

Goldie nodded. "I couldn't talk to you in your world," she explained, "but I understood what you were saying. All the animals here walk upright and talk, just like me."

The girls gazed around in delight. "A forest full of talking animals," said Lily.

"This is amazing!"

Goldie put her paws to her mouth and called, "Come out, everyone! Meet Jess and Lily!"

A little door between two tree roots opened and a mole peeked out. From another door came a squirrel wearing a bowtie. His tail swished as he hopped over to the girls. Door after door opened and more animals appeared, gathering around Lily and Jess.

"I'm Harry Prickleback," said a little hedgehog as he waddled out from a clump of candyfloss flowers.

"It's lovely to meet you," said Lily, bending down to tickle Harry's nose and making him giggle. She could hardly believe she was talking to a hedgehog!

A kitten wearing a rucksack scampered over. "I'm Bella Tabbypaw," she said.

"What kind of animal are you? You're too tall to be a rabbit and you haven't got any wings, so I don't think you're birds…"

"We're girls!" Jess stroked Bella under her soft chin. She could feel the rumble of her purr.

"None of the animals have seen people before," Goldie explained. "That's why they were hiding."

A bird almost as tall as the girls flapped down from a tree. "Captain Ace, at your service," he said. He wore a flying helmet with a badge reading *Ace Air Travel* and raised one wing in a salute.

"He's a stork!" Lily whispered to Jess. Jess saluted Ace back.

Two rabbits came out of the Toadstool Café, one in a waiter's jacket and one brushing flour from her apron. "Well, I say, how lovely to meet you!" said the waiter. "We're Mr and Mrs Longwhiskers."

Running out behind them came a young rabbit with a purple ribbon around her neck. She was so small that

Lily thought she'd fit in the palm of one

hand.

"I'm Lucy Longwhiskers," the rabbit said in a rush. "You're really tall. How old are you? Do you live in Friendship Forest like me? How—"

Goldie interrupted her with a laugh. "This is Lily and Jess's first visit to Friendship Forest. Would you like to help me show them around?"

Lucy gave a happy squeak. "Can I?

Can I?" she asked her mum and dad.

"Of course," said Mrs Longwhiskers. "Stay close to

Goldie, and don't get into any trouble!"

The animals bustled around as the girls waved goodbye.

"Bye!" squawked Captain Ace. "Come back soon!"

The girls glanced excitedly at each other as they set off through the trees with Goldie and Lucy. Sweet scents drifted up from the flowers and beads of dew twinkled on the mossy ground like tiny stars.

"You've been at Helping Paw before, haven't you, Goldie?" asked Lily as they walked. "We both recognised you. Why did you bring us here?"

"Ever since I was a tiny kitten, I've been able to go between Friendship Forest and your world," Goldie explained. "I was in your world when I hurt my paw, and a kind lady took me to your wildlife hospital."

Goldie told Lucy how Lily and Jess had looked after her while she recovered.

Lucy's eyes were wide and shining. "That was so kind! I'm happy that you're in Friendship Forest." She bounded on ahead.

"I never forgot you," Goldie said. "I've always thought that if I needed help,

I could call on you two."

"Are you in trouble, Goldie?" Jess asked. "What's wrong?"

"I think Friendship Forest is in danger." Goldie lowered her voice so Lucy wouldn't hear. "A few days ago, I was on my way home with a basket full of berries when I saw a tall woman in a cloak walking through the trees. I was about to say hello, but then she stopped to pick a flower. Its pretty yellow petals went grey, then it turned to dust in her hand!"

Lily gasped in shock. "How horrible!

But who was she?"

"I don't know." Goldie's whiskers trembled. "I'm worried she might harm Friendship Forest."

A shiver ran through Jess. They couldn't let that happen!

"Don't worry, Goldie," Jess said. "If this stranger tries anything, we'll stop her."

"You can count on us!" Lily said.

"Thank you," said Goldie, reaching up to hold the girls' hands in each of her forepaws. "Here we are! Welcome to my home!"

CHAPTER FOUR

Grizelda

The trees opened out to reveal a large, mossy clearing in front of a cave. Set into the front of the cave was a red door with a little window in the shape of the letter G.

Goldie beamed. "This is my grotto!"

Lucy hopped across the clearing, her

tiny white tail bobbing. "Look at the Blossom Briar!" she said, sitting on her back legs and peering up.

Lily and Jess followed Lucy's gaze. Growing beside the cave was a bush as tall as the forest trees. It was covered in huge, colourful flowers as fluffy as pompoms.

Lily gave a delighted cry. "It's beautiful!"

"The Blossom Briar is connected to every flower in Friendship Forest," Goldie explained. "As long as the Blossom Briar blooms, all the flowers in the forest will too."

Jess ran to stand beneath the Blossom Briar's branches, giggling as a football-sized yellow flower tickled her face. "It's like being inside a rainbow!" she called. She took out her sketchbook and started to draw the shape of the flowers.

Lily held Lucy up so she could sniff

a purple flower. The little rabbit was quivering with excitement.

Then Lily spotted something strange. An orb of yellow-green light was floating above the Blossom Briar.

"What's that?" Lily asked.

Goldie's eyes went wide with alarm. "I don't know, but I've got a bad feeling about it. My fur's standing on end!"

They all watched the light float down. It hovered in the centre of the clearing, casting an eerie glow. Lily could feel Lucy trembling in her arms.

"Quick, hide!" said Goldie. She pushed

open the red front door and they ran inside.

Through the window, the girls could see the orb of light growing bigger, then… *Cra-ack!* It exploded into a shower of green sparks.

The sparks faded to reveal a tall, thin figure wearing a shiny purple tunic over tight black trousers. Her high-heeled boots had sharply pointed toes, and her long green hair swirled around her head. A black cloak hung from her shoulders.

"It's the woman I saw!" Goldie whispered.

Jess felt her tummy tighten into a knot. She glanced at Lily. She could tell from her friend's wide eyes that she'd had exactly the same thought…

"Goldie," Jess said, "I think that woman is a witch!"

Goldie frowned. "A witch? What are witches?"

"Bad people who do magic," Lily said.

She felt an icy shiver ripple down her spine. "They're usually just in stories, but this one's real…"

Lucy squealed and ran to hide behind Goldie's bed.

Goldie swallowed. "Stay here."

She opened the door and stood in front of the witch. "You must leave Friendship Forest at once!" she cried.

The witch's thin lips curled into a smile, but her eyes glittered coldly. "I don't think so," she said with a sneer. "I've built a wonderful tower across the Wide Lake, full of darkness and cobwebs. When I climbed to the top, I saw this forest – and now I want it for myself!" She rubbed her hands together. "Of course, I'll have to get rid of all the animals first."

"No!" said Goldie bravely. "Friendship Forest is our home!"

Jess could see that the tip of Goldie's tail was trembling with fear. "We said we'd help Goldie," she told Lily. "Come on!"

Jess pushed open the door and the girls went and stood next to their friend.

"Goldie's right," Jess said, her fists clenched. "Witches don't belong here! Clear off!"

The witch peered down her thin nose at the girls. "Well, what have we here?" she said. "Two silly little human girls. You must be pretty stupid to think you can get the better of Grizelda!"

The witch laughed. The sound echoed around the clearing like terrible peals of thunder. Lily felt a cold wind whip around her.

"Friendship Forest will be mine and I know how to get it," the witch snapped.

"I heard what you said about the Blossom Briar, cat. Green is for hair, not leaves! I'll destroy it – then all the flowers in the forest will die. It will turn grey and miserable and all the animals will leave!"

Lily shuddered. She couldn't imagine Friendship Forest without its beautiful flowers. "We won't let you, Grizelda!" she

said, trying to keep her voice steady.

The witch gave another dreadful cackle. "You're too late. My servants are already here to start work!"

At that moment, four hideous, lumpy creatures the same size as Lily and Jess crashed through the trees. They wore filthy, ragged clothes, and their fur was a

patchwork of dingy green, washed-out blue and sickly yellow. They smelled like rotting cauliflowers.

Grizelda clapped her hands as the creatures gathered around her. "Welcome, Boggits – my messiest and most loyal servants. If you tear down the silly Blossom Briar, you can have that cave as your new home!" She turned to Goldie. "You'd better find somewhere else to live, cat. You and your humans can't stop me!"

And with that, Grizelda snapped her fingers and vanished in another shower of sparks.

CHAPTER FIVE

Bunny-napped!

The girls stared at each other in dismay. Then Goldie bravely walked up to the Boggits.

"I live in this grotto," she said politely. "But I'm sure we can find you a new home somewhere else."

The first Boggit shook his grubby head.

"Boggits been living in a mud pool by Grizelda's tower. This grotto be much better once Boggits make it good and messy!"

"But you can't steal Goldie's home!" Jess protested.

"Or hurt the Blossom Briar!" added Lily.

The second Boggit snorted. "Boggits not listen to nosy humans. I be starting with nasty flowers now."

"Ladies first, Pongo," growled a girl Boggit, elbowing him out of the way.

"Oi, Whiffy, that hurt!" yelled Pongo.

Whiffy took no notice. She jumped up at the Blossom Briar, ripping off a flower.

"Stop!" shouted Lily.

The Boggits just laughed. "Haargh! Haargh!"

"Now rip down them other flowers," shouted Pongo. "Come on, Sniff! Over here, Reek!"

"No!" shouted a little voice.

Lucy had come out of Goldie's grotto. The tiny rabbit's whiskers were quivering with fear, but she hopped up to the Boggits.

"Leave the Blossom Briar alone!"

cried the little rabbit.

"Lucy, go back inside!" called Goldie.

But before Lucy could move, Pongo

scooped the rabbit up in his big, smelly paw. Lucy squirmed, her ears shaking with fright.

"Help!" she squeaked.

Jess clenched her fists. "Put her down!"

Goldie sprang at Pongo, reaching out for Lucy. But the Boggit dodged aside.

"Go, Pongo!" Whiffy yelled. "We show rabbit what happens when you mess with Boggits."

Clutching Lucy, Pongo ran off.

"After him!" yelled Jess.

The girls and Goldie followed as Pongo crashed through the forest. But the Boggit had got a head start, and soon he was far ahead of them.

"This way!" called Lily, leading her

friends around a bush with white flowers that were shaped like stars. But when they reached the other side, Pongo had vanished among the trees.

Jess felt as if her heart had sunk into her trainers. "He could have taken Lucy anywhere. How will we know where to look?"

"There must be a clue somewhere," said Lily.

She peered around a tree while Goldie sniffed the air for his horrible, rotting smell.

"Nothing," the cat said.

Jess wriggled right under the bush, but there was no sign of Pongo or the little rabbit.

"Do you think he might have taken Lucy into our world?" Jess asked, rubbing mud from her leggings.

Goldie shook her head. "I can visit the human world because I was born there, but the other animals can't – and you're the only humans who can visit Friendship Forest." For a moment, her

worried frown faded and she smiled up at the girls. "Your love of animals makes you special, you see."

"So Lucy's somewhere in the forest," Jess said. "But where?"

Lily sat on a patch of moss, trying to think. Beside her, the star-shaped blooms nodded in the soft breeze. Most of them were as white as milk, but one was grey

– just like the flower Grizelda had turned to dust. Then another of the white blooms turned as dull as stone.

"Look!" Lily cried. "The flowers are dying because the Boggits are hurting the Blossom Briar."

With a gasp, Jess pointed to a patch of yellow flowers. Lots of them were grey too.

"This is terrible," said Goldie. "The sooner we find Lucy, the sooner we can stop the Boggits! If we don't hurry, all the flowers in Friendship Forest could die."

Nearly all of the star flowers were grey now. But Lily noticed that one of them still had a purple, silky centre…

Her heart racing, Lily picked out a scrap of material from the flower. "Look!" she cried. "This comes from Lucy's bow, doesn't it? The ribbon must be unravelling. Everybody look for scraps of purple fabric. The trail will lead us to Lucy!"

CHAPTER SIX

Mr Cleverfeather

The girls and Goldie darted through the forest. Lily spotted a second piece of material.

"This way!" she called.

Soon, Jess found a third strand, then Goldie saw another beneath a tall tree.

"This must be the right way," she panted.

But that was the last scrap they found.

Jess groaned. "I can't believe it! We were so close."

They were all wondering what to do when a loud buzzing sound from above made them jump.

Jess looked up. "Watch out!" she cried, as hundreds of dead leaves showered down from the tree.

"Do you think it's Grizelda?" Lily asked, looking up anxiously. The thought of the witch lurking nearby made her shiver.

Buzzzz!

More leaves tumbled down. Jess darted away and leaned against a tree. Beneath her fingers, she felt the trunk move…

Jess spun around. The surface of the trunk was rippling and twisting!

"Hey, look at this!" she called.

Lily and Goldie hurried over. A staircase appeared on the tree, winding around the trunk up into the branches.

"More magic!" Lily breathed.

"Maybe Lucy's up there," Jess suggested. "Let's find out!"

She put one foot on the bottom step and began to climb, with Goldie and

Lily close behind.

At the top, Jess called down, "There's some sort of shed up here!"

"Did you say a shed?" asked Lily, amazed.

"Yes," said Jess. "The door's open. Perhaps Lucy's inside!"

Goldie and Lily followed Jess into the ramshackle treehouse. The girls

had to stoop slightly because their heads touched the ceiling. It was gloomy, with leaves everywhere, and no sign of Lucy…

But there was an owl. He wore a striped waistcoat with lots of little pockets, and a monocle fixed in front of one eye, like half a pair of spectacles.

"Yeeeek!" the owl screeched. He pressed a lever on the long tube he held.

Buzzzz! It blew the leaves into a spin, making the girls and Goldie squeal.

"Yeeeek!" the owl screeched again. He dropped the tube and his monocle flew off.

"Don't be scared!" cried Goldie. "It's me, Goldie, and my friends, Lily and Jess!"

The owl felt around the floor with his wing tips. "Where's my monocle?" he wailed. "I can't see properly without it."

Lily found it and gave it to him.

"Thank you," he said. "I do jolly pies."

"Jolly pies?" Jess wondered aloud.

"I think he means 'apologise'!" said Lily.

"Girls, this is Mr Cleverfeather," Goldie explained. "I think we've found his secret inventing shed!"

The girls gazed around. Half-finished gadgets, drawings and tools covered every surface. A diagram labelled *For Twinkletail Family* showed plans for a double-decker pushchair that held five baby mice on each level. Another was a machine for catching baby birds that fell out of their nests.

"What's the long tube for?" asked Lily, pointing to the contraption that Mr Cleverfeather was holding.

"It's my latest invention," Mr Cleverfeather said. "A beef laster. Er, I mean a leaf blaster. Leaves get everywhere, you see, and mess up my inventions." He squinted at Jess and Lily. "What sort of creatures are you?"

"Jess and Lily are young humans," Goldie explained. "They're clever and brave."

"Most interesting," said Mr Cleverfeather. "But why are you here?"

Goldie told him about Lucy, the Boggits and the Blossom Briar.

"Have you seen Lucy?" Lily asked.

"I'm afraid not," said Mr Cleverfeather.

Lily wasn't surprised. He didn't seem to have very good eyesight.

"You could try my telescope," Mr

Cleverfeather suggested. "Maybe you can spot the runny babbit – er, bunny rabbit." He opened the back door and led them onto a balcony.

Mr Cleverfeather lifted a cover made of leaves stitched together, revealing a wooden telescope. Lily crouched down to look through it, scanning the forest in all directions. Suddenly, she caught sight of something moving at the top of a chestnut tree.

"It's Lucy!" she yelled. "But she's in a cage. Her ears are droopy and she looks so sad."

Jess and Goldie gasped as they took turns to look through the telescope at the little rabbit.

Faintly, Lucy's voice floated towards them. "Help! Please, someone help me!"

"She's really scared!" Goldie cried.

Jess clenched her fists. "Let's get her out of there, right now!"

"But she's so high up in that tree," Lily said despairingly. "We'll never reach her!"

CHAPTER SEVEN

Boggit Blaster

"Ahem. There is a way," said a voice.

"Mr Cleverfeather!" said Jess, turning to see the owl standing behind them.

"You can use my pea-shoot laugh," Mr Cleverfeather explained. "I mean, my secret path. Ta-da!" He swished back a curtain of willow fronds, revealing

a wooden path covered in vines that snaked through the treetops.

"A walkway!" cried Lily.

"It helps me get around," said Mr Cleverfeather. "My old wings aren't what they used to be."

Thanking Mr Cleverfeather, Goldie, Jess and Lily ran off along the walkway, grabbing the wooden railings to keep their balance. Soon they were close enough to see Lucy huddled in a cage made from sticks and rope.

"Help!" Lucy whimpered.

"We're here, Lucy!" Goldie called. "We'll get you out!"

When she saw them, Lucy's ears perked up. "Goldie and the girls! Hooray!" she shouted, hopping about on her tiny paws.

When they reached the cage, Jess tugged at the ropes that held the bars together – but they wouldn't budge. Lily and Goldie tried too, but the ropes remained firmly tied.

Lucy's ears drooped back down. In a trembling voice, she asked, "Will I have to stay here forever?"

"Of course not!" said Lily. "We're going to save you." But she gave Jess and Goldie a worried look. How could they free the little bunny?

Goldie was examining the knots that held the ropes in place. "Pongo has done these up really tightly. We need something to loosen them…"

Jess felt a fizz of excitement as an idea came to her. She took her pencil out of her shorts pocket and worked the tip into the bunched-up knot.

Goldie's green eyes gleamed as the knot fell apart. "Brilliant, Jess!"

Jess took one end of the rope, Lily the other, and together they undid the cage. The sticks came apart and Lucy bounded out onto the walkway.

"You rescued me!" she cried, her white tail bobbing as she hopped around their feet. "Thank you, Goldie! Thank you, girls!"

Lily kneeled down to pick Lucy up. She curled up in the crook of Lily's arm, her whiskers twitching happily.

They hurried back to Mr Cleverfeather's tree, where the owl gave a delighted squawk. "Young Lucy! I'm so happy to see you wit and fell – er, fit and well."

Goldie's tail drooped. "We've rescued Lucy," she said, "but how can we stop the

Boggits before they completely destroy the Blossom Briar?"

Jess gave a cry of excitement. "I've got an idea! Mr Cleverfeather, can we borrow your leaf blaster?"

Hiding behind a bush next to Goldie's Grotto, Jess got the leaf blaster ready. A horrible smell filled the air, like filthy pond water mixed with stinky trainers and mouldy cheese. Through the bush's leaves, they could see the Boggits stomping around the Blossom Briar. Many of its flowers had been

ripped down and lay trampled around the clearing.

Lucy trembled in Lily's lap and folded her ears over her eyes.

"Don't worry," Lily whispered. "We'll keep you safe."

Sniff's dirty, multicoloured fur bounced as she clambered onto Whiffy's back so she could reach more flowers. She tore down a red one, yelling, "This be good Boggit fun!"

Reek jumped up and gripped a branch of the Blossom Briar that was covered in yellow flowers. With a creak it snapped under his weight. "Haargh! Haargh!" Reek laughed. He threw the branch into the clearing, where Pongo jumped up and down on it, crushing the petals.

Goldie's eyes flashed. "I think we've seen enough," she whispered. "Hurry, Jess!"

Jess pressed the leaf blaster's lever.

Buzzzz!

SWOOOSH!

A gust of air blew, sending trampled petals into a rainbow-coloured whirlwind spinning around the Boggits.

"Uggy! Uggy!" Pongo cried.

"Nasty flowers in my fur!" shrieked Sniff. "Get them off!"

Reek yelled in panic. "Beastly petals in my pants!"

"Pooh! I smell like flowers!" Whiffy roared, brushing off blossoms. "Disgusting! Boggits must get out of here!"

Lily, Jess and Goldie giggled. Even Lucy peeped out when Jess gave another quick blast, making the Boggits shriek.

"What's happening?" Lucy asked.

"The Boggits like dirt and nasty smells," Lily whispered, "so if we smother them with pretty flowers, they'll go away."

Buzzzz!

The shrieks and yells grew louder.

"Boggits, back to Grizelda's tower!" Pongo bellowed. "Bath in mud pool will take nasty flower smells away."

The horrible creatures thundered off into the trees.

"Hooray!" yelled Jess and Lily. Goldie reached up and grabbed their hands, spinning them round in delight, while Lucy hopped beside them, her tiny white tail bouncing.

Then Jess noticed a familiar orb of yellow-green light was zipping through the trees towards them…

Goldie's fur stood on end. "Grizelda!"

CHAPTER EIGHT

Watch Out, Grizelda!

The orb of light burst into a storm of angry yellow sparks that faded to reveal Grizelda. Her green hair flicked and twisted like snakes.

Lucy dived back beneath the bush, but Jess, Lily and Goldie stood their ground.

"Don't think that you've defeated me!"

the witch screeched. "You've stopped the Boggits this time, but I'll find a way to take Friendship Forest for myself!"

Jess's legs were trembling but she stepped forwards. "It won't work, Grizelda," she said. "Whatever you try, we'll stop you!"

Grizelda stooped down low and narrowed her eyes. When she spoke, Jess could feel her cold breath. "Two girls and a cat are no match for me," she hissed. "You had better watch out!"

She snapped her fingers and disappeared in another flash of sparks.

After a moment's silence, Lily spoke. "Actually, it's Grizelda who had better watch out."

Jess nodded. "We'll help keep Friendship Forest safe, Goldie."

The cat slipped a paw into each of their hands. "I knew I was right about you two," she said, smiling. "Come on, let's take Lucy home."

"And the Boggits ran away, covered in petals," said Jess, finishing the story of their adventure to all the animals at the Toadstool Café.

Mr and Mrs Longwhiskers pulled Lucy into a hug. "Thank you so much for rescuing her," Mr Longwhiskers cried.

"Hooray for Goldie and the girls!" chanted Harry Prickleback and Bella Tabbypaw. "They stopped the witch!"

The other animals joined in while

Captain Ace the stork flew a loop-the-loop above them.

Mrs Longwhiskers disappeared into the café to make a celebration tea, while Mr Longwhiskers asked about the poor Blossom Briar.

"In time, its blossoms will grow back," Goldie said. "I'm afraid some of the flowers in the forest have been damaged, but most of them are safe."

After a little while, Mrs Longwhiskers called, "Tea's ready!"

The café tables were laden with delicious food. Mr Longwhiskers poured blackberry juice and strawberry fizz into acorn cups. They ate honey sandwiches and rolls filled with watercress, button tomatoes and sweet radishes. Next were slices of iced seed cake with cherries on top. Mrs Longwhiskers said that the cakes were only biscuit-sized for Lily and Jess, so they must have a whole one each!

Just as they were feeling full, Captain Ace spluttered into his cup of strawberry fizz. He'd spotted Mr Cleverfeather coming out through the trees. "Well, I never!" the captain said. "We hardly ever see Mr Cleverfeather these days!"

“A big cheer for Mr Cleverfeather and his leaf blaster,” shouted Jess. “Hip, hip…”

“HOORAY!”

Jess gave the leaf blaster back to Mr Cleverfeather, and the old owl pressed the lever by mistake, showering Lucy with cake crumbs.

"I say," said Mr Cleverfeather, "I do, er—"

"Jolly pies!" said Goldie, and everyone laughed while Lucy nibbled at the crumbs. Lily gave the owl a plate of sandwiches and seed cake.

"What a day!" Jess said, munching on her cake.

"It was amazing," agreed Lily. "But I think my mum will be wondering where we are. It's time for us to go home."

They said goodbye and Goldie led them to a beautiful tree with golden leaves close to Toadstool Glade.

"This is the Friendship Tree," Goldie said. When she touched a paw to the trunk a door appeared, just like the one in Brightley Meadow.

Lily looked serious. "Goldie, I think Grizelda meant what she said. She won't stop trying to make the animals leave the forest."

Goldie sighed. "You're right," she said. "She'll find another way to harm the forest. Maybe she'll

attack the Silver Spring where the river starts, or the Treasure Tree, where we get our food…"

"Then we'll stop her," said Jess fiercely. "We promise!"

Goldie hugged each of the girls. "Thank you," she said. "As soon as Grizelda makes trouble again, I'll come and find you."

Lily opened the door in the tree.

"Goodbye, Goldie!" the girls chorused. "See you soon!"

They stepped into shimmering golden light. As it cleared, they found themselves back in Brightley Meadow.

"Did that really happen?" asked Lily.

"I think so," said Jess.

They glanced back. The door had disappeared, but they could still make out the letters carved into the tree trunk.

"It wasn't a dream," Lily murmured. "Friendship Forest is real."

"It must be so late," said Jess, checking her watch. She frowned. "Hey! It's the same time as when we left!"

Lily stared. "So time stood still while we were in Friendship Forest? Cool! Listen, Jess," she said. "Shall we keep this our secret?"

"Of course!" said Jess. "Our very own magic animal friends. Who would believe us, anyway?"

They laughed and skipped over the stepping stones, back to the wildlife hospital. As they walked through the gate, Lily's mum waved at them.

"Having a good morning?" she asked.

"Yes, thanks," said Lily. "The best start to the holiday ever. So far it's been—" She looked at Jess.

They giggled and said together, "Magical!"

The End

Grizelda is still trying to take over Friendship Forest and now her horrid Boggits have played a mean trick on little Molly Twinkletail!

Join Lily, Jess and Molly in the next adventure,

Molly Twinkletail Runs Away

Turn over for a sneak peek . . .

Jess and Lily both drew a sharp breath. The Boggits were talking about Molly Twinkletail!

Pongo thumped his chest. "Pongo was clever, telling her to fetch drinks from Sparkly Falls for Boggits."

Sniff laughed so much she nearly fell out of the tree. "Off mouse run to help. But mouse will never be able to do it. Haargh haargh!"

The Boggits whooped and jumped onto the ground. They ran around the Treasure Tree trunk, kicking squashed fruit at each other.

Jess, Lily and Goldie stared at each other in alarm.

"Poor Molly," said Lily. "She just wants to help people – even the horrible Boggits. Now she's even further from home. And all alone!"

Read

Molly Twinkletail Runs Away

to find out what happens next!

Magic Animal Friends

Read all the Magic Animal Friends adventures and be part of the secret!

Series One

COMING SOON!

Look out for
Jess and Lily's
next adventure –
with adorable puppy
Poppy Muddlepup!

3 stories in 1!

www.magicanimalfriends.com

Puzzle Fun!

Can you spot the five differences between the two pictures of Lucy Longwhiskers?

ANSWERS

1. Spot on toadstool missing
2. Whisker missing
3. Extra star and sparkle
4. Grass missing to Lucy's right
5. Tail of her bow is missing

Lily and Jess's Animal Care Tips

Lily and Jess love helping lots of different animals – both in Friendship Forest and in the real world.

Here are their top tips for looking after...

RABBITS

like Lucy Longwhiskers

- If you have a pet rabbit, make sure they don't get bored by hiding treats around their cage and giving them lots of toys to gnaw on.

- Don't forget to give your rabbit fresh water daily and the right food to keep them healthy.

- Make your rabbit's hutch cosy and fun by making lots of hideaway holes for them to snuggle up in – just like they would in the wild.

- If you are concerned about a poorly-looking wild bunny, ring your local wildlife animal hospital.

Lily's parents aren't the only ones who run a wildlife hospital.

Have you heard of Tiggywinkles – the world's busiest wildlife hospital? They take care of over 10,000 poorly animals every year and treat all kinds of wildlife, including hedgehogs, badgers, birds, foxes and deer.

If you are worried about a wild animal, you can have a look at their website for hints and tips about what to do.

www.tiggywinkles.com

Orchard Books supports Tiggywinkles.

Magic Animal Friends

Can you keep the secret?

There's lots of fun for everyone at www.magicanimalfriends.com

Play games and explore the secret world of Friendship Forest, where animals can talk!

Join the Magic Animal Friends Club!

- Get special gifts
- Exclusive content
- All the latest Magic Animal Friends news!

To join the Club, simply collect all four tokens from the books in series one and send them in to us.

Don't forget to:
1) Include your name and address
2) Include the signature of a parent or guardian

Send your tokens to:
Magic Animal Friends Membership Offer,
Orchard Books Marketing Department
338 Euston Road, London, NW1 3BH

Terms and Conditions
(1) Open to UK and Republic of Ireland residents only (2) Purchase of Magic Animal Friends books is necessary (3) Please get the signatur of your parent/guardian to enter this offer (4) The correct number of tokens must be included for the offer to be redeemed (5) Photocopie tokens will not be accepted (6) Membership packs are distributed or first come, first served basis whilst stocks last (7) No part of the offe is exchangeable for cash or any other offer (8) Please allow 28 days delivery (9) We may use your data to contact you with further membership offers (10) Prizes may vary from pictures shown. We reserve the right to offer prizes of an alternative or greater value